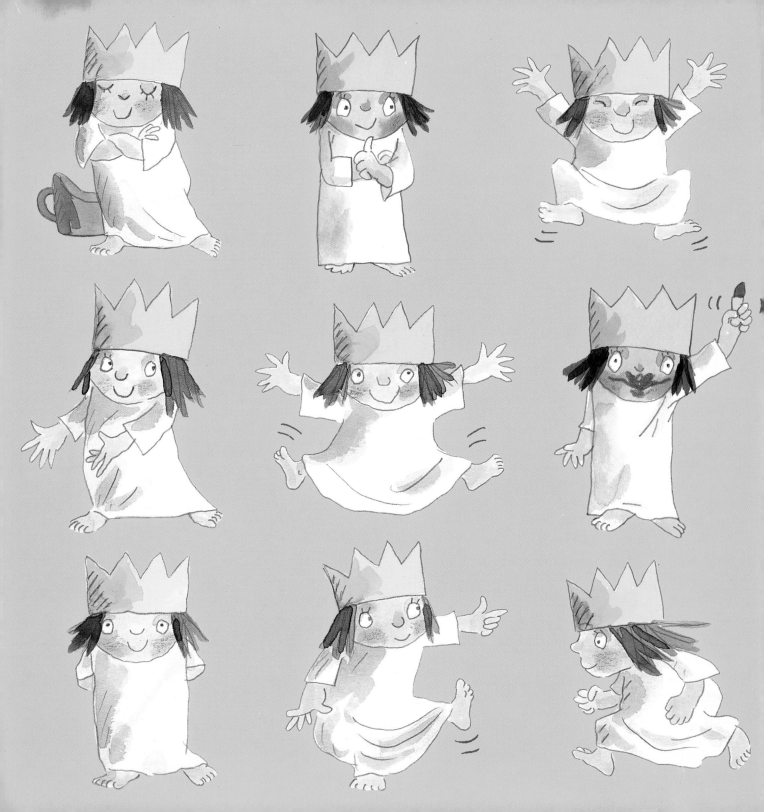

With my thanks to San Kiu Lieu and Samantha Riches
who gave me the idea for this story and their
permission to use it when they were at
Keyworth Primary School in London

First published in hardback in Great Britain by Andersen Press Ltd in 1999
First published in paperback by Picture Lions in 2000
This edition published by Collins Picture Books in 2001

3 5 7 9 10 8 6 4

ISBN: 0-00-664730-8

Picture Lions and Collins Picture Books are imprints of the Children's Division, part of HarperCollins Publishers Ltd.

Text and illustrations copyright © Tony Ross 1999, 2001

The author/illustrator asserts the moral right to be identified as the author/illustrator of the work.

A CIP catalogue record for this title is available from the British Library.

The HarperCollins website address is: www.fireandwater.com

Printed in Hong Kong

I Want A Sister

Tony Ross

Collins

An imprint of HarperCollins*Publishers*

"There's going to be someone new in our family,"
said the Queen.

"Oh goody!" said the Little Princess.
"We're going to get a dog."

"No we're not," said the King.
"We're going to have a new baby."

"Oh goody!" said the Little Princess.
"I want a sister."

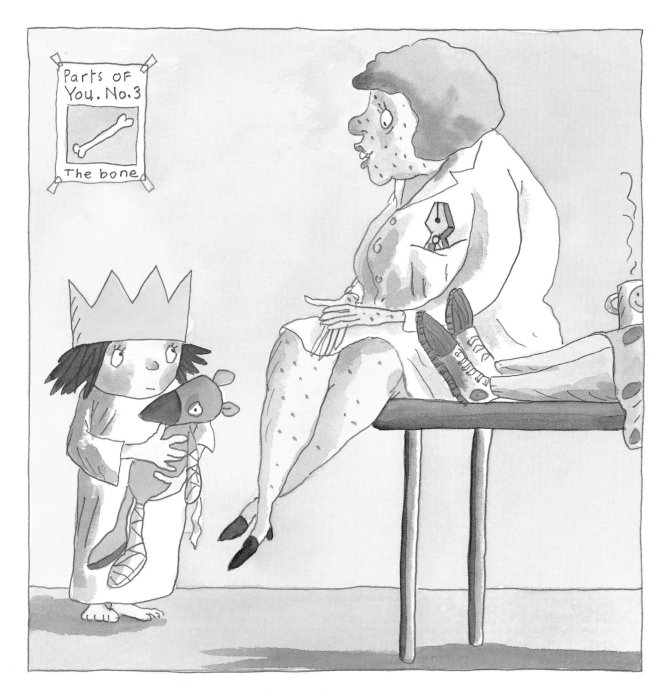

"It may be a brother," said the Doctor.
"You can't choose, you know."

"I don't want a brother," said the Little Princess.
"Brothers are smelly."

"So are sisters," said the Maid.
"Sometimes you smelled AWFUL."

"I don't want a brother," said the Little Princess. "Brothers are rough."

"So are sisters," said the Admiral.
"Both make TERRIFIC sailors."

"I don't want a brother," said the Little Princess.
"Brothers have all the wrong toys."

"Brothers' toys can be just like yours,"
said the Prime Minister.

"Well," said the Little Princess,
"I JUST DON'T WANT A BROTHER."

"Why?" said everybody.
"BECAUSE I WANT A SISTER," said the Little Princess.

One day, the Queen went to the hospital
to have the new baby.
"Don't forget… " shouted the Little Princess,

"... I WANT A SISTER!"

"What if it's a brother?" said her cousin.

"I'll put it in the dustbin," said the Little Princess.

When the Queen came home from hospital,
the King was carrying the new baby.

"Say 'hello' to the new baby," said the Queen.
"Isn't she lovely?" said the Little Princess.

"He isn't a she," said the King. "You have a brother.
A little Prince!" "I don't want a little Prince,"
said the Little Princess. "I want a little Princess."

"But we already have a BEAUTIFUL little Princess,"
said the King and Queen.
"WHO?" said the Little Princess.

"YOU!" said the King and Queen.

"Can my brother have this,
now I'm grown up?"
said the Princess.

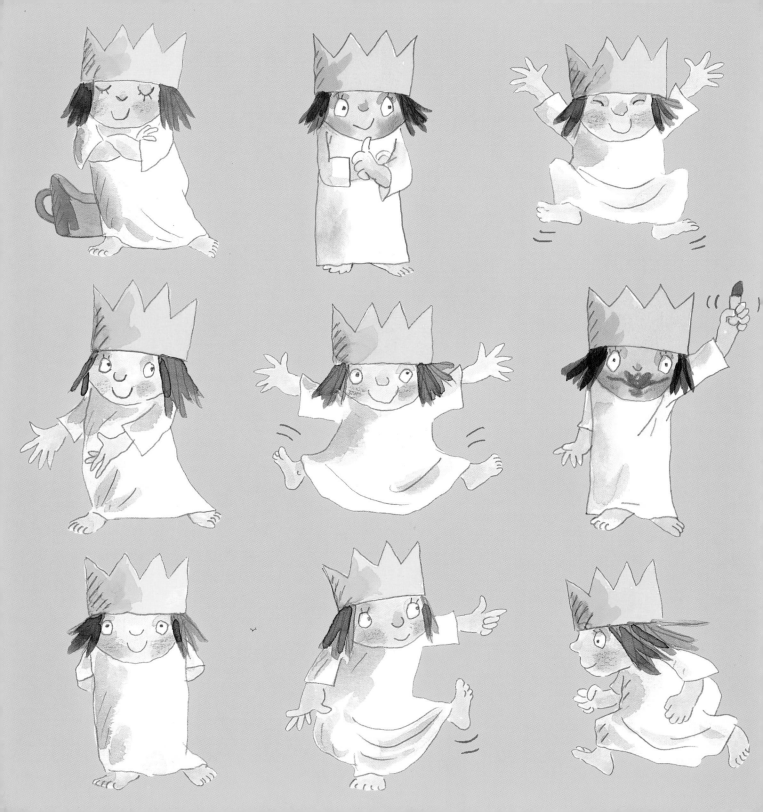

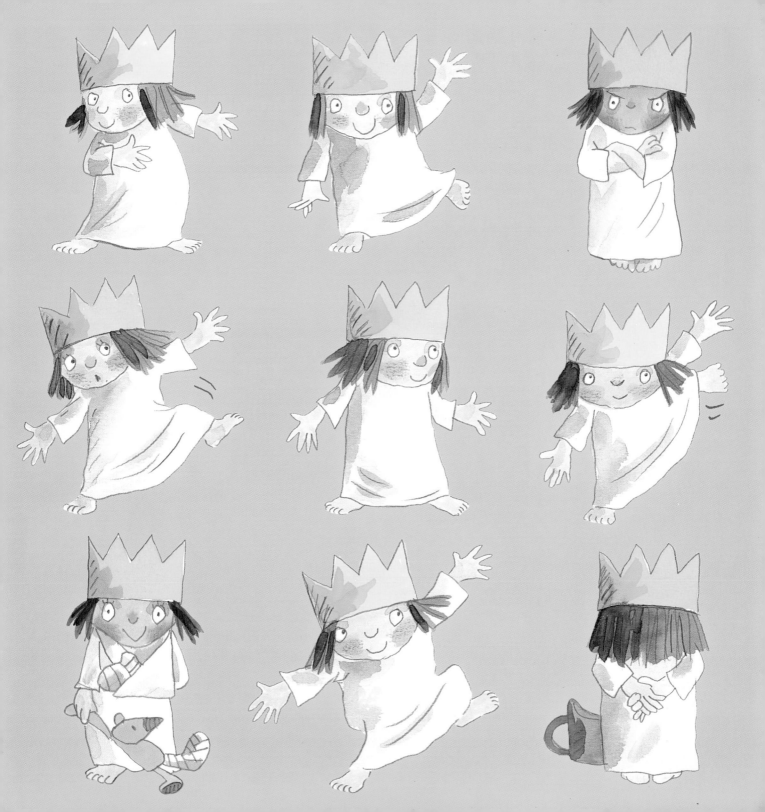

Collect all the funny stories
featuring the demanding
Little Princess!

0-00-662687-4 — I Want My Potty / Tony Ross

0-00-664357-4 — I Want To Be / Tony Ross

0-00-664356-6 — I Want My Dinner / Tony Ross

0-00-664730-8 — I Want A Sister / Tony Ross

0-00-710957-1 — I Don't Want To Go To Hospital / Tony Ross

Tony Ross was born in London in 1938. His dream was
to work with horses but instead he went to art college
in Liverpool. Since then, Tony has worked as an art
director at an advertising agency, a graphic designer,
a cartoonist, a teacher and a film maker – as well as
illustrating over 250 books! Tony, his wife Zoe and
family live in Macclesfield, Cheshire.